First published in the United States, Canada, Great Britain, Australia, and New Zealand in 1996
by North–South Books, an imprint of Nord–Süd Verlag AG, Gossau Zürich, Switzerland.
Distributed in the United States by North–South Books Inc., New York.

Library of Congress Cataloging-in-Publication Data is available.
A CIP catalogue record for this book is available from The British Library.
ISBN 1-55858-658-X (trade binding) 10 9 8 7 6 5 4 3 2 1
ISBN 1-55858-659-8 (library binding) 10 9 8 7 6 5 4 3 2 1
Printed in Belgium

For more information about our books, and the authors and artists
who create them, visit our web site: http://www.northsouth.com

A Michael Neugebauer Book
North–South Books / New York / London

HENRY & HORACE CLEAN UP

By Wolfgang Mennel
Illustrated by
Gisela Dürr
Translated by
Marianne Martens

At Horace's house everything was perfect, and
Horace was feeling very pleased with himself.
He had cleaned every room, done the laundry,
weeded the garden, and mowed the lawn.
Now he was enjoying a well-deserved rest and
a cold glass of lemonade.

"Ahhh, this is the life," he thought. He would
have stayed like this, nice and comfortable, but . . .

Across the street at Henry's house everything was a mess, and Henry was feeling quite miserable. He sat on his treasure chest and looked around. In the middle of his living room there was a lawn mower and a broken bicycle. There were shoes all over the place, and Henry couldn't even sit on his sofa because it was so cluttered.

It was just too much of a pigsty—even for a pig.

"That's it. I've got to clean this place from top to bottom. But where do I begin?" thought Henry.

Then Henry had an idea. "First I need to clear everything out so it will be easier to work," he said. "There's lots of room at Horace's." He picked up a flowerpot and carried it across the street.

"I'm cleaning my house. Mind if I put my flowerpot here while I work?" Henry asked.

"No problem," said Horace.

"May I leave my other flowerpots here too?"

"All right. Just put them in my garden," said Horace.

"Thanks," said Henry. "Would you mind giving me a hand?" Together they walked over to Henry's house.

"Could you carry this chair for me?" said Henry. "It's so-o-o
heavy, and you are so-o-o strong."
"Well, yes, I suppose I am," said Horace, flattered.
"And would you mind grabbing that floor lamp?"
"Well, uh, all right."
"And when you come back, you could get that chest of
drawers and the television—and . . .

the washing machine,
the fishbowl,
the coat rack,
the telephone,
the umbrella,
the clock,
the bicycle,
the watering can,

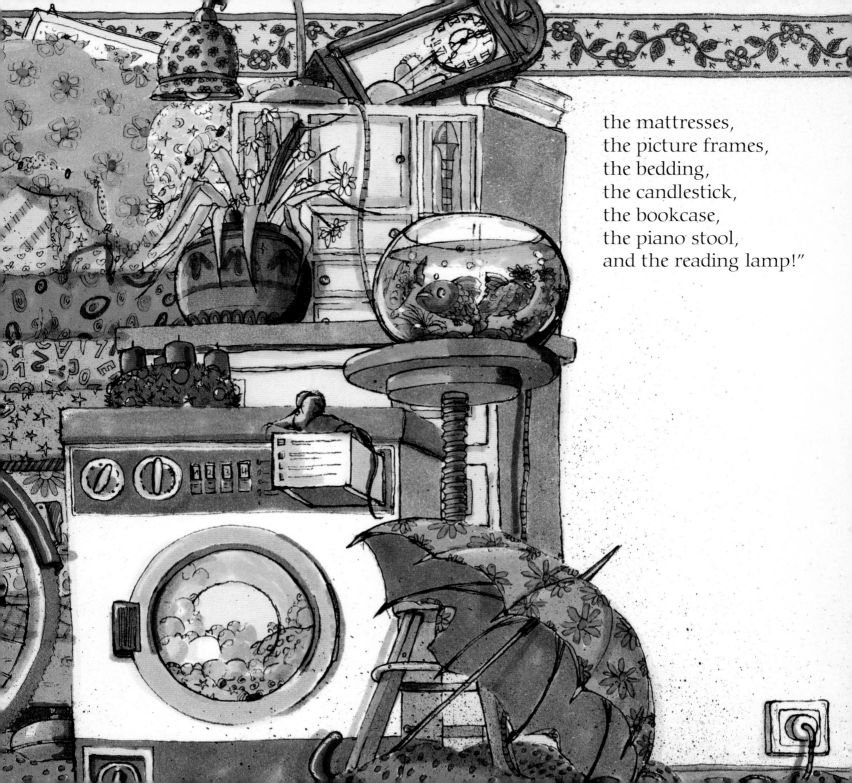

the mattresses,
the picture frames,
the bedding,
the candlestick,
the bookcase,
the piano stool,
and the reading lamp!"

"You're the strongest elephant in the whole wide world!" Henry
shouted. "But I bet you can't carry my treasure chest."
"Oh, of course I can," bragged Horace as he threw the chest up
on his shoulders. "What's in here, anyway?"
"It's a secret," Henry whispered.
"It's a really heavy secret!" said Horace.

"Hey—what are you going to carry?" Horace asked.
"Why, I'm going to run ahead and show you the way!" answered Henry.

Horace sighed.

Finally all of Henry's things were in Horace's garden. But Henry still wasn't happy. He sat on the couch and thought for a minute.

"What if it starts to rain? It would really be a lot better to put everything inside your house," he said to Horace.

So poor Horace dragged all of Henry's things into his house.

Meanwhile, back at Henry's all the mess was gone.
"Actually, it doesn't look bad at all," thought Henry. "The floor needs to be scrubbed and the walls need a fresh coat of paint, but I'm sure Horace won't mind helping. I'll go and ask him right now."

Suddenly, from Horace's house came a loud crash and then a sad trumpeting sound.

Henry raced
across the street.

The house was
so crammed with
junk that he
couldn't find
Horace anywhere.

Henry began to dig, and after a lot of hard work he finally freed Horace and helped him outside.

Horace collapsed onto the grass, crying.
"Well, you certainly were lucky," Henry said. "If it hadn't been for me, you might still be stuck."
Horace shook his head sadly. "No. If it hadn't been for you, I would be sitting peacefully in my nice clean house in my comfortable chair, drinking lemonade."
Henry was suddenly very quiet. He looked embarrassed.

"I'm sorry, Horace," he said. "Don't cry. Tomorrow I'll fix everything. And tonight we can camp out! Come on, it will be fun!"

That night Henry and Horace sat
in front of a crackling fire, roasting ears of
corn and watching the stars together. When they
had finished eating, Henry turned to Horace.
"Thank you for all your help today," he said. "You are
a good friend—such a good friend that I'm going to show you
my secret treasure." And with that, Henry opened the chest.

The two friends sat up far into the night sharing
the treasure by the light of their campfire.